UNITED STATES
SUPREME COURT
LIBRARY

Chief Justice William Rehnquist

by Bob Italia

Published by Abdo & Daughters, 6535 Cecilia Circle, Edina, Minnesota 55439.

Photo credits: A/P Wide World Photos-cover, 11, 23, 29
Globe Photos-5, 24
UPI/Bettmann-8, 12, 17, 19, 20, 23

Edited by: Paul Deegan

Library of Congress Cataloging-in-Publication Data

Italia, Robert, 1955-
      Chief Justice William Rehnquist / written by Bob Italia ; [edited by Paul Deegan].
          p. cm. — (Supreme court justices)
      Includes index.
      Summary: A career biography of the sixteenth Chief Justice of the United States.
      ISBN 1-56239-096-1
      1. Rehnquist, William H., 1924- —Juvenile literature. 2. Judges—United States—
Biography—Juvenile literature. [1. Rehnquist, William H., 1924- . 2. Judges. 3. United States.
Supreme Court—Biography.] I. Deegan, Paul J., 1937- . II. Title. III. Series.
KF8745.R44I83 1992
347.73'2634—dc20
[B]
[347.3073534]
[B]
                                               92-13709
                                               CIP
                                               AC

Table of Contents

Page

4   The 16th Chief Justice of the United States

6   "I'm Going to Change the Government"

7   A Talent for Law

10 Rehnquist becomes Political

15 Nominated to the Supreme Court

21 A Controversial Justice

27 Rehnquist becomes Chief Justice

31 Setting America on a New Course

33 How Rehnquist Views Himself and the Court

36 The Private Side of William Rehnquist

38 What the Rehnquist Court Holds for the Future

39 Glossary

40 Index

The 16th Chief Justice of the United States

William Rehnquist is one of the most influential and controversial Chief Justices of modern times. Throughout his legal career, Rehnquist's conservative views have led him to support some of the most unpopular causes and issues of our time. In 1953, Rehnquist favored racial segregation and limiting the rights of criminals. Today, he opposes abortion and granting more rights to minorities and women.

Justice William H. Rehnquist, Associate Justice of the United States Supreme Court since 1972.

Though he has his share of critics, William Rehnquist remains one of the country's most brilliant legal minds. And he will fight hard against any one—even the President of the United States—when Constitutional rights are threatened.

"I'm Going to Change the Government"

William Rehnquist was born October 1, 1924, in Milwaukee, Wisconsin. His father was a paper salesman who never went to college. His mother was a housewife who graduated from the University of Wisconsin in Madison. She was very active in the community and could speak five languages.

Rehnquist's father was a dedicated Republican. His conservative political views would influence Rehnquist throughout his life. An elementary school teacher once asked Rehnquist what he wanted to do when he grew up. Rehnquist replied: "I'm going to change the government."

A Talent for Law

After graduating from high school, Rehnquist received a scholarship from Kenyon College. But during his first year he dropped out. World War II was raging in Europe, and Rehnquist felt obligated to do his part for his country. In 1943, he enlisted in the Army Air Corps where he worked in the meteorology program. He then served in North Africa for the remainder of the war.

In 1945, Rehnquist enrolled at Stanford University in Palo Alto, California. There he studied political science. He graduated in 1948 and immediately went to graduate school at Harvard. After a year at Harvard, Rehnquist returned to Stanford to study law. He eventually graduated at the top of his Stanford Law School class in 1952.

Supreme Court Associate Justice Sandra Day O'Conner was Rehnquist's classmate at Stanford Law School. She recalled that Rehnquist was "head and shoulders above all the rest of us in sheer legal talent and ability."

Rehnquist's success in law school paid off immediately. Supreme Court Associate Justice Robert Jackson named Rehnquist as one of his law clerks. (Of the thousands of law school graduates each year, only a few are chosen to become Supreme Court clerks). After his clerkship, Rehnquist moved to Phoenix, Arizona, to begin his own legal practice.

William Rehnquist (back row-far left) poses with his graduating class at Stanford.

Rehnquist becomes Political

In Phoenix, Rehnquist became active in the Republican party. He made many speeches criticizing then Supreme Court Chief Justice Earl Warren. Rehnquist believed Warren, considered a "liberal," was "making the Constitution say what he (Warren) wanted it to say."

Rehnquist did not like the way Warren favored protecting the rights of criminals. He also did not like the way Warren expanded the power of the Federal government, and encouraged government regulation of business. Rehnquist opposed these beliefs.

Rehnquist gives a speech.

In 1954, the Supreme Court ruled in *Brown vs. Board of Education* that racially segregated public schools were unconstitutional. That meant whites and blacks could attend the same public schools, and that public schools for whites only and blacks only were against the law.

Of this historic decision, Rehnquist said in 1985, "I think there was a perfectly reasonable argument the other way." Rehnquist wrote in 1952 that the existence of public schools segregated by race was "right and should be reaffirmed by the Supreme Court." But the Court ruled otherwise.

In 1964, Rehnquist joined the presidential campaign of Republican Senator Barry Goldwater. Goldwater was running against President Lyndon Johnson. Rehnquist worked hard and traveled throughout Arizona. He urged people to vote for Goldwater. Though Goldwater lost, Rehnquist had established himself as an influential Republican spokesperson. His efforts helped launch his legal career.

Deputy Attorney General Richard Kleindienst (l) and Assistant Attorney General William Rehnquist, 1970.

In 1968, Republican Richard M. Nixon became President of the United States. Nixon named Richard Kleindienst, a Phoenix lawyer and Republican leader, as Deputy Attorney General. Kleindienst then brought William Rehnquist to Washington, D.C.

Rehnquist was appointed head of the Justice Department's Office of Legal Counsel. Rehnquist had become the President's lawyer's lawyer. He traveled the country, making speeches on behalf of President Nixon's programs and views.

Rehnquist drew criticism when he spoke in favor of mass arrests of Vietnam War protesters. But he also earned the respect of Congress for his presentations on such issues as campaign reform, obscenity, and wire-tapping.

"Rehnquist was so well prepared and well spoken that he could make the right wing (conservative) positions sound resonable to the liberal Congressional committee," said one member of the House of Representatives. "He was effective because there was almost nothing of the rightwing zealot about him. He was too good a lawyer for that."

*W*illiam Rehnquist owes Richard Nixon for his appointment to the Supreme Court. But Rehnquist's appointment was not due to Nixon's ability to choose a good candidate. Rehnquist joined the Court because Nixon chose the wrong candidate.

In 1971, aging Supreme Court Justices Hugo Black and John Harlan retired because of health problems. Nixon had to appoint two new justices. But before Nixon's choices could be confirmed, they had to be approved by the Senate. The Constitution requires that the Senate give its "advice and consent" to such appointments. Approval is usually a routine matter.

President Nixon's first choice was Clement Haynsworth, a conservative judge from Georgia. But the Senate rejected Haynsworth, claiming a conflict of interest.

Nixon chose Harrold Carswell, a conservative judge from Florida. But the Senate also rejected Carswell, questioning his moral character. (Carswell was later arrested on morals charges).

Now President Nixon was under a lot of pressure to find more qualified Supreme Court candidates. He chose Lewis Powell, a respected Democratic lawyer from Richmond, Virginia. Powell had a sparkling legal and personal record. He would have no problems being appointed. But that still left one vacant position on the Court. Who else could Nixon choose?

President Nixon with his two new Supreme Court Justices— Lewis Powell (l) and William Rehnquist (r).

One of Nixon's aides half-heartedly suggested William Rehnquist. Rehnquist was not well-known outside the Nixon administration. He was young for a Supreme Court nominee. But he had political experience, was very conservative, and had a reputation as a good lawyer.

The Senate could find little fault with Rehnquist. The only black mark against him was that he was accused of harrassing black voters in a 1964 Phoenix election—charges Rehnquist denied.

The sixteen members of the Senate Judiciary Committee voted 12 to 4 to continue Rehnquist's appointment. Then the entire Senate approved of Rehnquist, 68 to 26. William Rehnquist was one of the youngest Supreme Court Justices ever. He officially took his seat on the Court in January, 1972.

Supreme Court Justice William Rehnquist.

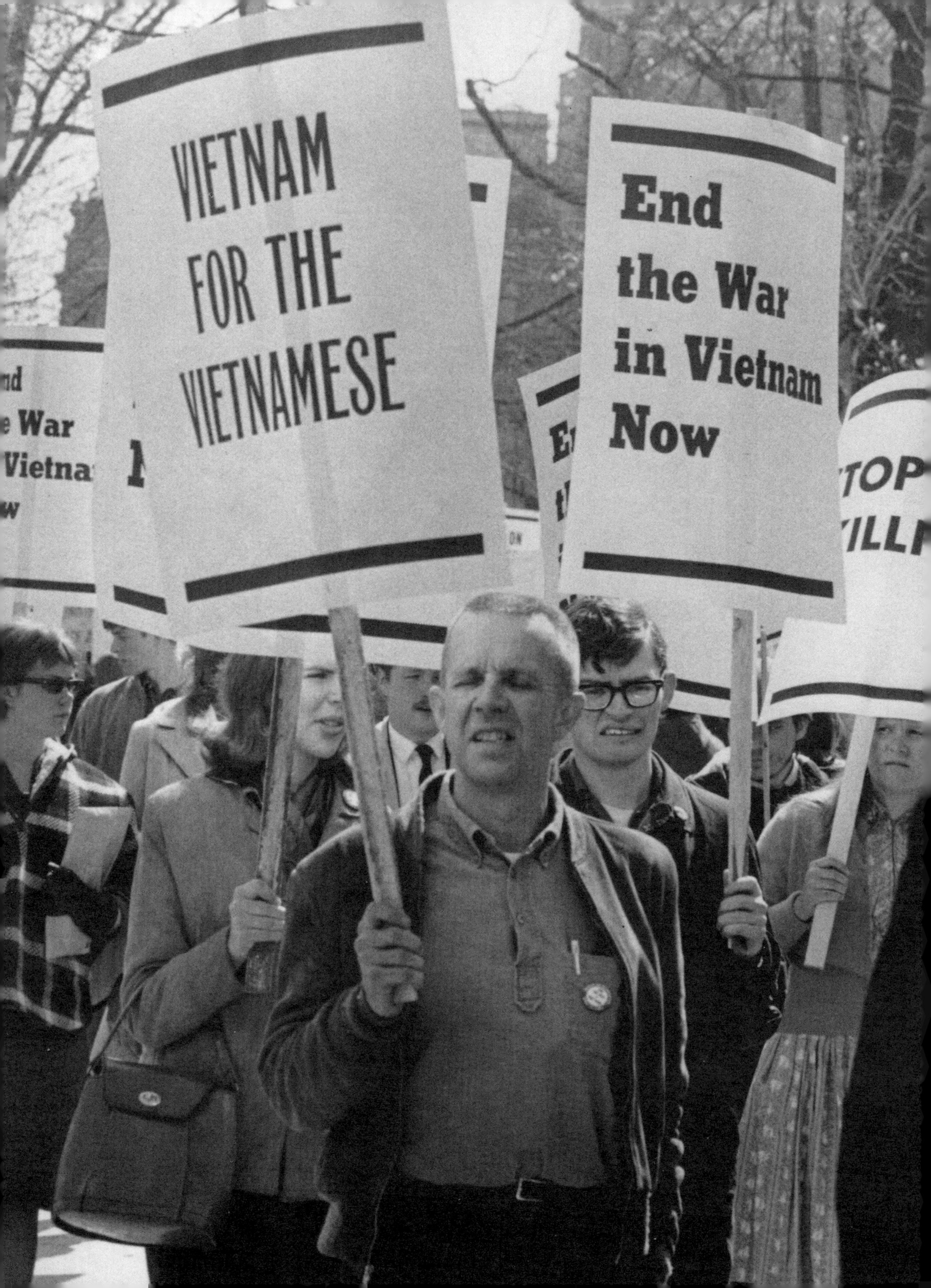
VIETNAM FOR THE VIETNAMESE
End the War in Vietnam Now

A Controversial Justice

Almost immediately, Rehnquist got himself into trouble. The Supreme Court was reviewing an emotional legal case. Antiwar activists challenged a surveillance program the Pentagon was conducting.

Many people felt Rehnquist should have disqualified himself from the case when it came to the Supreme Court. He had previously testified against the activists when he was with the Justice Department. But Rehnquist did not disqualify himself. He cast the deciding vote against the activists.

5,000 students picketed in front of the White House on April 17, 1965, to protest the Vietnam war.

In another case, Senator Mike Gravel of Alaska approached the Supreme Court. He was seeking the right to print some top-secret government papers about the Vietnam war. (They were called the Pentagon Papers).

When Rehnquist was an assistant attorney general in the Justice Department, he originally organized the government's lawsuit to stop the publication of the Pentagon Papers. Again, many people felt he should have disqualified himself from the case. But he did not— and eventually cast the deciding vote against Senator Gravel.

President Nixon points to the transcripts of the White House tapes after announcing they would finally be made public.

When President Nixon refused to surrender the White House Watergate tapes, the case reached the Supreme Court. Rehnquist finally disqualified himself. But he did so without any explanation.

Rehnquist identified himself as controversial and conservative, yet consistent. He voted against desegregation of schools. He voted in favor of public aide to private schools. He saw nothing wrong with religious exercises or prayer in public schools, nor with Nativity scenes on public property.

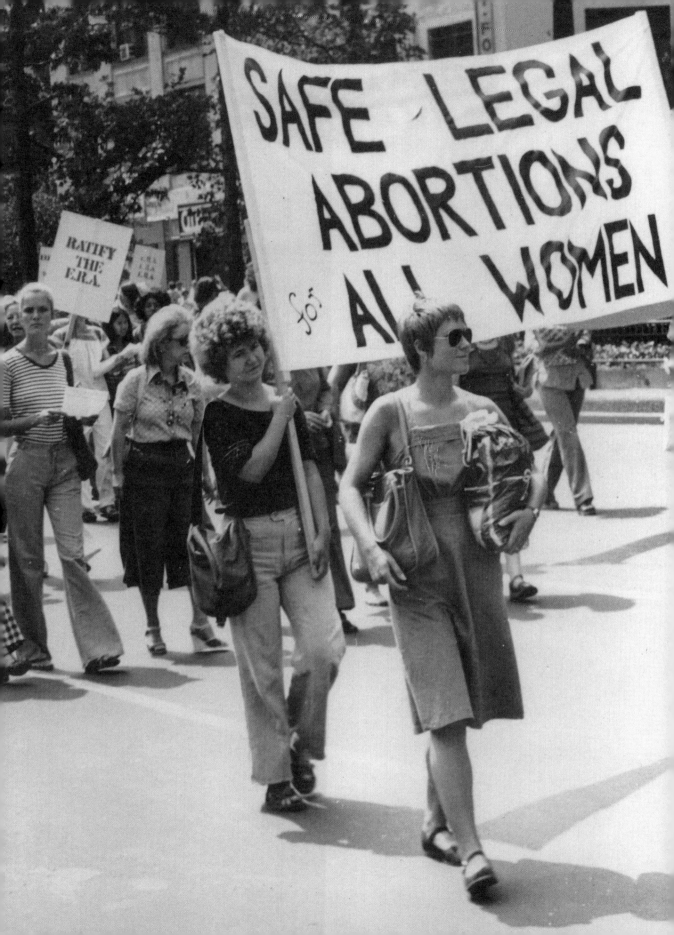

He voted against expanding Constitutional rights for blacks, women, criminals, and the news media. And he worked hard to limit access to the Federal courts by those who believed their Constitutional rights had been violated. Rehnquist did not oppose the death penalty, nor was he against the use of illegally-obtained evidence in court.

Rehnquist also developed a reputation for being a Supreme Court "dissenter." A dissenter is a justice who goes against the majority opinion of his or her fellow justices.

In 1973, Rehnquist dissented from a decision that legalized abortion. In 1976, Rehnquist dissented from a decision that laws treating men and women

Pro-abortionists demonstrate in New York.

differently must be legally examined. In 1980, he dissented from a ruling requiring states to conduct trials, in most situations, that are open to the public.

And in 1981, he dissented from the Supreme Court's decision to review a murder conviction, which he claimed would encourage more appeals and delay the death sentence.

By the time President Ronald Reagan nominated him as the Chief Justice, Rehnquist had filed 54 solitary dissenting opinions— opinions not one of his eight fellow justices shared. No justice before him had filed as many dissenting opinions. In recognition of this fact, his clerks presented Rehnquist with a small statue of the Lone Ranger. Rehnquist displays the statue proudly in his Supreme Court office.

Rehnquist becomes Chief Justice

In June 1986, Chief Justice Warren Burger retired from the Supreme Court. He wanted to devote his time organizing the Bicentennial celebration of the Constitution. Now President Reagan had to appoint a new Chief Justice of the Supreme Court.

Usually a new Chief Justice is appointed from outside the Court. Rarely is an associate justice moved into the top spot. Such an appointment can create bad feelings amongst the other justices. They might resent being passed up for the position.

Reagan suprised many court observers when he nominated William Rehnquist as Chief Justice of the Supreme Court. (Reagan also annouced at the televised White House ceremony that he was nominating Antonin Scalia to take Rehnquist's place as an associate justice. Scalia was later approved by the Senate.)

Immediately, civil rights groups and women's groups opposed Rehnquist's nomination. They did not like Rehnquist's conservative views. They promised to fight the nomination.

Rehnquist's past came back to haunt him. Again he was accused of harassing black voters when working as a Republican pollwatcher in the 1960s. But Rehnquist testified under oath that he had never harrassed or intimidated voters.

On September 26, 1986, Rehnquist (l) takes the oath of office from retiring Chief Justice Warren Burger. Rehnquist's wife Nan holds the Bible.

The Senate took three months to confirm Rehnquist's nomination. The Judiciary Committee voted 13 to 5 in his favor. The full Senate, after an exhausting four-day debate, voted 65 to 33 to confirm him.

Up to that time, no nominee for a Supreme Court position had ever received 33 negative votes. And no previous Chief Justice had ever been approved by less than a 2 to 1 margin. But all the negative voting did not bother Rehnquist. "I am looking forward to the future and to trying to be a good Chief Justice," he said.

Setting America on a New Course

During Rehnquist's first term as chief justice, 1986-87, the Supreme Court remained moderate in their decisions. Some people had feared a swing in the Court's decision-making. Decisions favoring women's rights, affirmative action, free speech and the separation of church and state were made despite Rehnquist's known opposition.

During the 1987-88 term, the Rehnquist Court remained unusually moderate. In one case, Rehnquist himself ruled that a Central Intelligence Agency (C.I.A.) employee, who was fired because he was a homosexual, had the right to challenge that action in court. And he ruled against a decision that granted the Reverend Jerry Falwell a $200,000 award from a magazine Falwell claimed had ruined his good name.

But by his third term, 1988-89, Rehnquist's conservative views began to assert themselves. The Court granted permission to states to restrict abortion. The Court set laws making it more difficult for workers to file race and sexual discrimination suits against employers. And the Court also restricted affirmative action plans and limited the rights of criminals.

"It is now truly the Rehnquist Court," said one newspaper reporter. "As chief justice, Rehnquist presides like a fine conductor. The musicians might play the same notes without him, but his clear direction and distinctive style are unmistakable."

As chief justice, Rehnquist also sets policy for all the country's federal courts.

How Rehnquist Views Himself and the Court

William Rehnquist is proud of his conservative views and his record of dissent.

"If you think of a judicial conservative as one who generally inclines against broad interpretations of the Constitution," he said, "then I think I am a judicial conservative. I am also a strong believer in pluralism. Don't concentrate all the power in one place. And, you know, this is partly what the (Constitutional) framers also conceived. So it is a kind of line where political philosophy joins judicial philosophy. You don't want all the power in the government as opposed to the people. You don't want all the power in the federal government as opposed to the states."

Rehnquist does not believe in tampering with the separation of powers set up in the Constitution. He prefers that the Court not actively seek out issues to examine.

"We're carrying out a Constitutional function that is a very delicate one," he said. "Every time that we say a law of Congress is unconstitutional, that a state law is unconstitutional, we are overriding a democratically reached decision. Now the Constitution requires us (the Court) to do that, but it requires us to do it only with great caution.

"I don't know that a court should really have a sense of mission," he added. "I think the sense of mission comes best from the President or the House of Representatives or the Senate. They're supposed to be the motive force in our government. The Supreme Court and the Federal judiciary are more the brakes that say, 'You're trying to do this, but you can't do it that way.' The idea that the Court should be way out in front saying, 'Look, this is the way the country ought to go,' I don't think that was ever the purpose of the Court.

"The justices of the Supreme Court were not appointed to roam at large in the realm of public policy and strike down laws that offend their own ideas of what laws are desireable and what laws are undesireable," he continued. "Justices of the Supreme Court have a great deal of authority, but it is not an authority to weave into the Constitution their own ideas of what is good and what is bad."

The Private Side of William Rehnquist

Most Supreme Court Justices are very private people. They rarely grant interviews and usually do not allow anyone to observe them at work. There is a Court policy that imposes strict judicial silence. Communication with the public usually comes through written opinions or speeches. Conservative William Rehnquist is no exception to these policies.

William Rehnquist lives with his wife, Natalie, in Arlington, Virginia. The Rehnquists have three children, all of whom have grown and are living their own adult lives throughout the United States.

In his free time, Rehnquist likes to paint landscapes. He also enjoys a monthly poker game with some of his closest friends. The Rehnquists have also been known to read classic fiction aloud to each other.

William Rehnquist will take time to play tennis doubles with his clerks once a week.

He also hold a sing-along each year for all his clerks.

Rehnquist has been described by those who know him as a friendly, witty, and charming person. He has an easy manner about him and dislikes formality. "Don't call me Chief," he told his fellow justices. "I'm still Bill."

What the Rehnquist Court Holds for the Future

Many observers believe that the 1988-89 term, when Rehnquist began asserting his conservative influence, will set the tone for the Rehnquist Court for many years to come. A justice's appointment to the Court is for life. Rehnquist will head the Court for many years to come.

Since President Bush continues to choose conservative justices, Chief Justice Rehnquist will have more colleagues who share his ideas about how the Constitution should be interpreted.

The Chief Justice has recognized that he does not control the votes of the eight associate justices. As Rehnquist once said: "They are as independent as hogs on ice."

Glossary

Abortion: Expulsion of a human fetus during the first 12 weeks of gestation.

Civil Rights: The rights of personal liberty guaranteed to U.S. citizens by the 13th and the 14th amendments to the Constitution.

Constitution: The lawmaking body of the United States of America.

House of Representatives: The lower house of Congress. Assembly for making laws in the United States.

Justice: The determination of rights according to the rules of law.

Segregation: The separation or isolation of a race, class or ethnic group by discriminatory means.

Senate: A governing or lawmaking assembly. The Congress of the United States is the Senate and the House of Representatives.

United States Supreme Court: The highest court in the United States, which meets in Washington, D.C. It consists of eight associate justices and one chief justice.

Vietnam: A country in Southeast Asia.

Watergate: Apartment and office building in Washington, D.C., that was the site of a cover-up scandal during Richard Nixon's administration.

Index

Abortion-25,32

Brown vs. Board of Education-10

Burger, Warren-27

Civil Rights-28

Constitution-6,10,25,27,33,34,38

Harvard-7

House of Representatives-14,34

Justice Department-14,18,22

Nixon, Richard-13,15,16,22

Reagan, Ronald-26,27

Rehnquist, William-4,6,7,9,10,13-
16,18,21,22,25-28,31-33,36,38

Senate Judiciary Committee-18,28,34

Senate-16,18,28

Stanford-7

Supreme Court-10,11,15,16,18,21,22,25-
28,31,32,34,36,38

Vietnam-14,18

Warren, Earl-10

Watergate-22